WHERE'S WALRUS?

BY STEPHEN SAVAGE • SCHOLASTIC PRESS • NEW YORK

FOR DAVID
THANKS TO ELIZABETH, JOE, RICCARDO,
AND MOST OF ALL, STEFANIE

All rights reserved. Published by Scholastic Press,
an imprint of Scholastic Inc., *Publishers since 1920.*
SCHOLASTIC, SCHOLASTIC PRESS, and associated logos are
trademarks and/or registered trademarks of Scholastic Inc.

Library of Congress control number: 2010922375
ISBN 978-0-439-70049-8
10 9 8 7 6 5 4 3 2   12 13 14 15
Printed in Singapore 46   First edition, February 2011

The artwork was drawn and created in Adobe Illustrator.
The title type was hand-lettered by Stephen Savage. The display
type and text type were set in Eunoia Regular and Gotham Book.
Book design by Stephen Savage and David Saylor

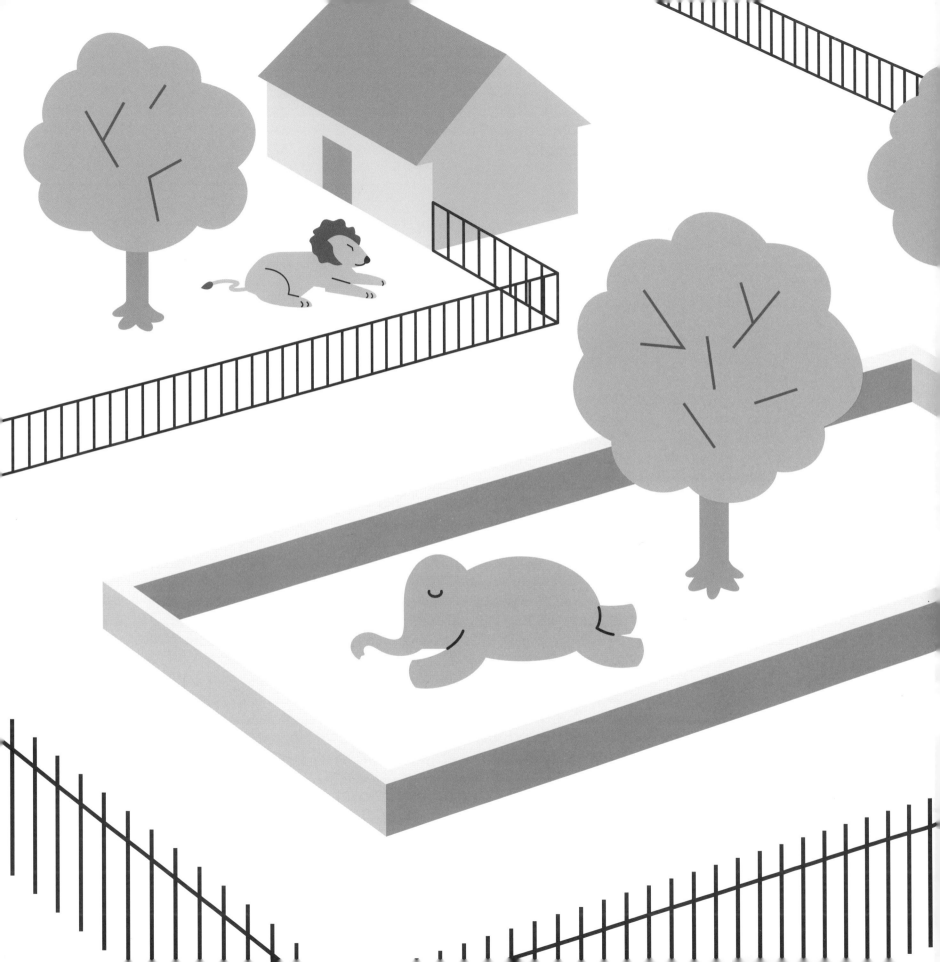

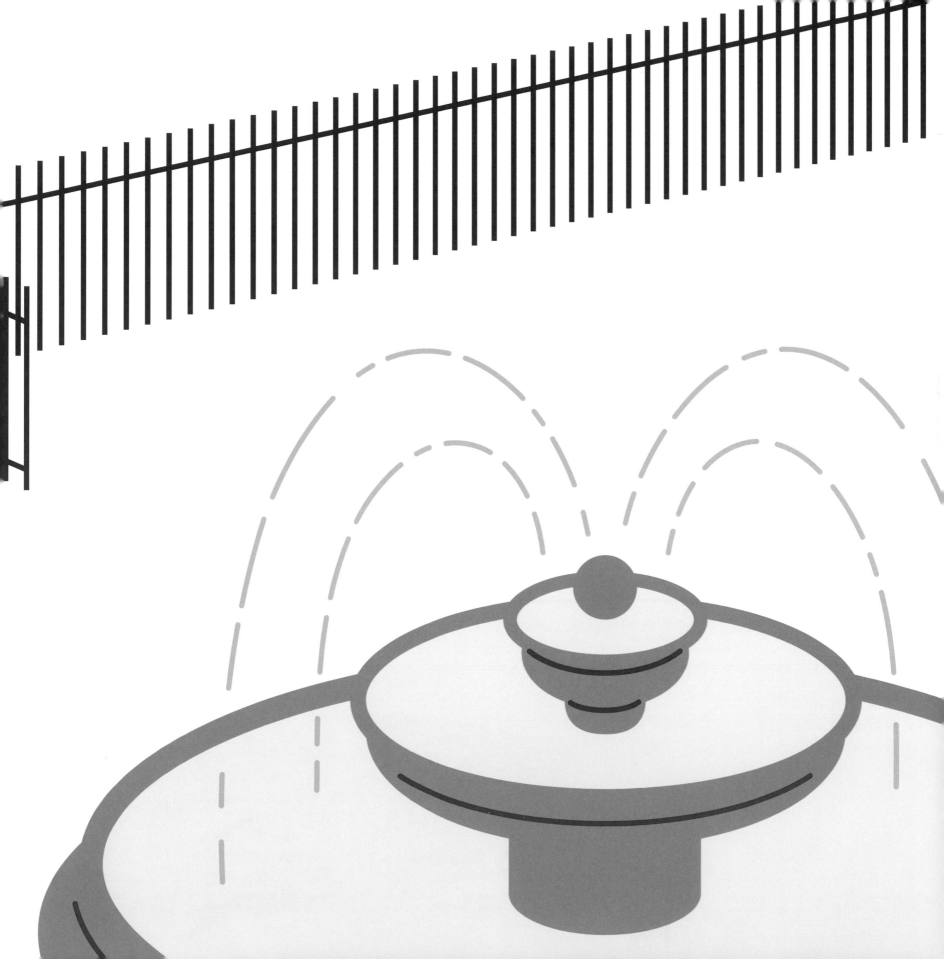

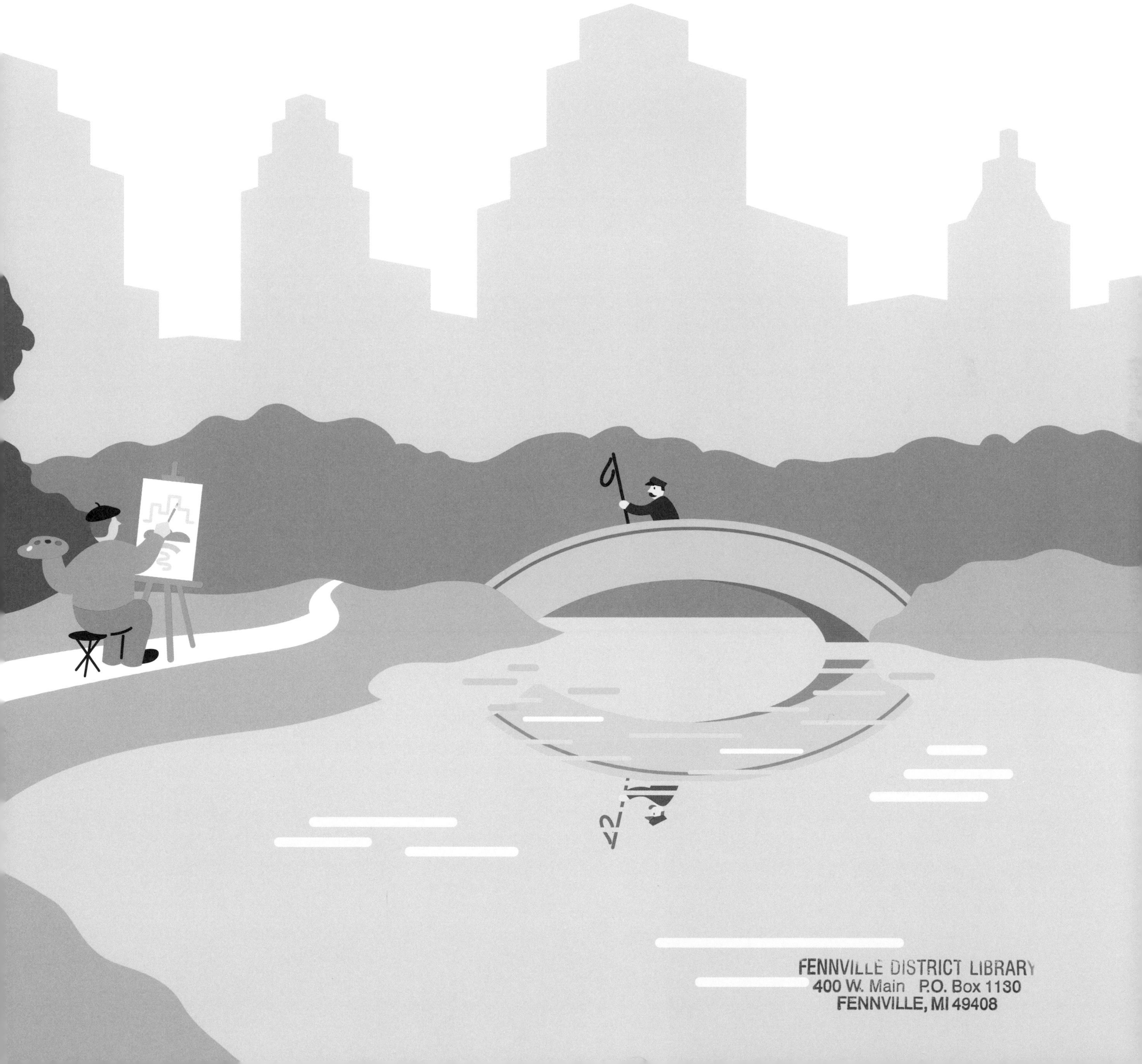

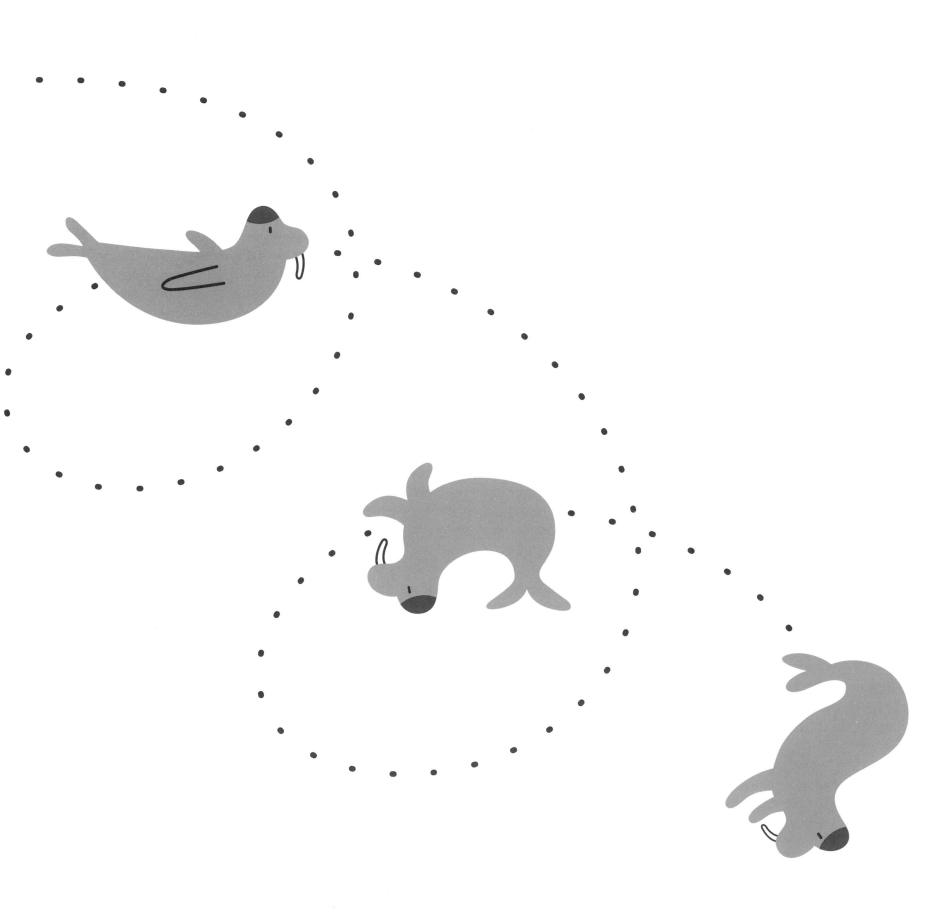

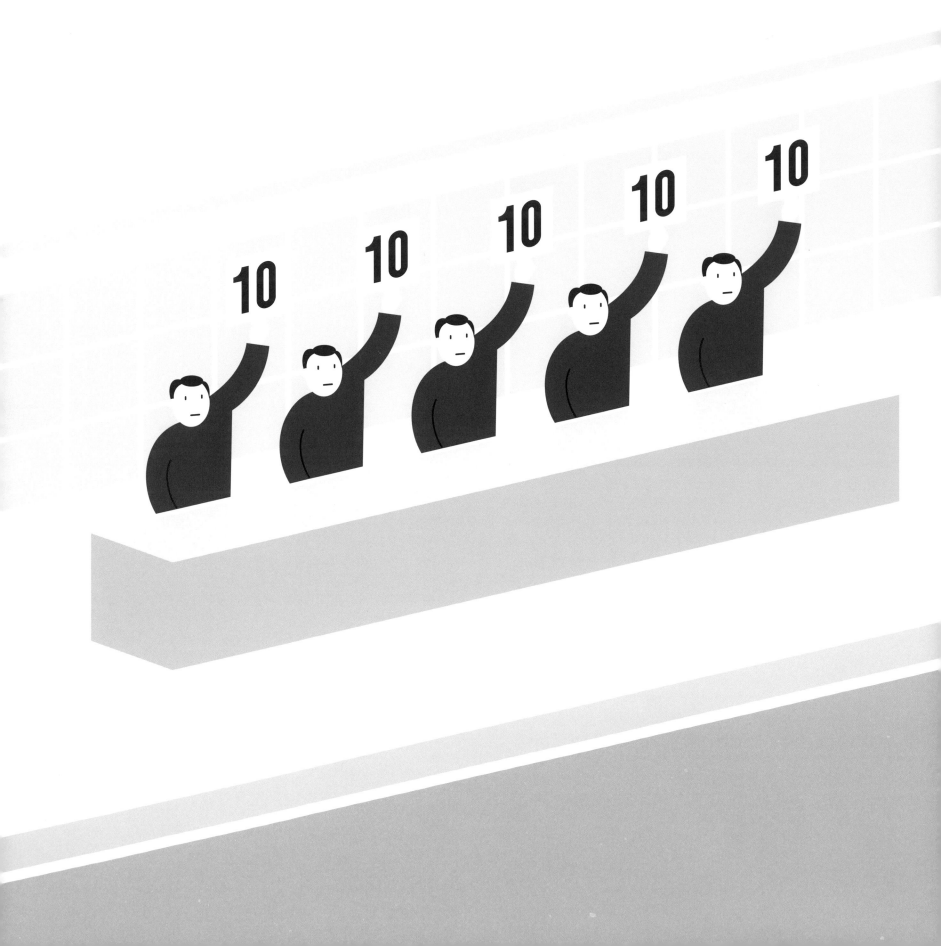